Chronicles Of The Imagination

GIFTED

D.Z. Adams

Published by
Zoheret Books

Library and Archives Canada Publication Data
Names: D.Z. Adams
Title: Chronicles of the Imagination – Gifted
Description: First Edition
Identifiers: ISBN 978-0-9938957-5-3

First Edition: April 2017

Contents

GMO – Genetically Modified Organism

Also known as Genetic Engineering is the process of forcing genes from one species into another unrelated species thus breaching the natural barrier between them.
Examples of GMOs include strawberries and tomatoes infused with fish genes to protect the fruit from freezing, goats crossed with spider genes to produce milk proteins stronger than Kevlar, dairy cows injected with a genetically engineered hormone to increase milk production, and rice infused with human genes to produce pharmaceuticals.
The injected genes can come from bacteria, viruses, insects, animals or humans…

Chapter 1

Dr. Gloria Walker stood in the semidarkness of the gestation room. The long row of artificial wombs glowed eerily in the blue lights emanating from the units. There was a constant hissing and gurgling as the units cycled synthetic embryonic fluids.

Gloria closed her eyes and took a deep breath enjoying the peace of the early morning hour. Soon the silence would be interrupted by classical music, followed by an hour of Chinese, then Jazz music, whale song and dolphin sounds. After an hour of silence, English, French, German, and Spanish filled the rest of the program. This regiment was designed to boost brain power in the fetuses during development.

Gloria's serenity was suddenly interrupted by a loud, high-pitched alarm. One of the units was failing. Gloria walked up to the womb and checked the vitals. With a sigh, she turned off the womb and gazed at the embryo. It was dead.

She walked to the next unit. The fetus within was moving. She connected her tablet to the womb's console and downloaded the data it had collected. In this way she worked her way along the row from unit to unit. By the time she got to the end, she had powered down five of the twenty wombs. She had not expected some of the embryos to live. The GMOs were too grotesque to be viable, but the death of fetuses that looked almost human and were close to the end of gestation was disappointing. She knew there would be at least one autopsy to attend this afternoon. She headed back to her office to prepare a report and call for cleanup. The units required sterilization before reseeding.

When Gloria entered her office, the phone was ringing. She picked up the receiver. "Hello?"

"Gloria, please come to my conference room immediately. It's urgent."

She felt a knot in her stomach as she made her way to the director's office.

When she arrived, she found all her colleagues present, some more disheveled than others. Everyone was equally confused at the sudden summons so early in the day.

Gloria was the last to take a seat.

"I've just had a call from our sponsor," the director said.

"There is no easy way to break this news to you," he continued, running a hand through his hair.

"We've been shut down."

At first this announcement was met with stunned silence. Then everyone spoke at once.

He held up his hand.

"The new administration was informed about the human GMO project and doesn't want to have anything to do with it. We are to shut down and close up shop."

"What about the embryos?" Gloria asked.

The director shook his head.

"We are to power off all units and hand over the data."
"But some are close to birth!" Gloria protested. "We can't just kill them!"
"You knew the deal when you signed on," the CEO said. "You were told the project could come to an end at any time. Well, it has. I want an update on the units by tomorrow morning. Dismissed!"

Gloria left the room in a daze. She had a hard time digesting the news.
"What a shit show!" a voice behind her said. She looked up into the troubled face of her elderly colleague Dr. Walter Snow.
"I know." She felt tears burning her eyes.
"Bloody hell," Walter said. "What are we goanna do?"
"Not sure what we can do." Gloria shook her head in disbelief.
For the past three years, Gloria and Walter had seeded and reseeded artificial wombs with an assortment of GMOs. They were not privy to the actual genetic engineering. That was done at a different security level in another department. They only received the zygotes and tried to keep them alive as long as possible. At first, they had assumed they were trying to find a cure for cancer. Later they had realized this was not the case when the fetuses received in vitro brain surgery.
Without further conversation, Gloria and Walter headed to the gestation room.
"Let's do this together," Gloria said.
They entered the dimly lit room and closed the door. The stereo was playing Beethoven's sixth symphony,

Gloria's favorite. She shut it off. The subsequent silence was deafening.

Gloria picked up the tablet used to collect the data and approached the first unit. The creature inside was growing a second set of arms and was close to fifty percent into its gestation.

Gloria plugged in the tablet and nodded at Walter who hesitated before powering off the system. They stood quietly and watched. A few minutes later it was over.

For the next hour they worked in grim silence shutting down unit after unit. Thankfully, most embryos had been seeded recently and were not too far along. Some were so deformed that it was unlikely they would have lived.

They came to the last womb. It contained a fully grown specimen ready for birth, the scar from the brain surgery still vividly red and visible through the embryonic fluid.

Gloria looked at Walter.

"I need a break and a coffee," she said.

Walter smiled at her diversion tactic. "Sure. Let's go." They left the room and locked the door.

"Are the units ready for cleanup?" Jorge, one of the cleaning crew, stood in the hallway with his cart.

"No, not for a while yet," Walter answered. "We'll give you a shout when we're ready."

Gloria felt a deep sense of gratitude towards Walter. "Where will you go when this is all over?" She asked him.

"Not sure. Maybe I'll retire. I suspect they'll give us a decent payout."

"Let's hope so," she said.

They allowed themselves half an hour before returning to the gestation room. It was quiet now that only one artificial womb was still operational. Without the glow from the units, they had to turn on the ceiling lights. Their brightness hurt the eyes. Gloria dimmed them to the lowest setting.

They approached the last functional unit. The specimen looked almost human. It floated in eerie silence with closed eyes sucking on one of its hands. Gloria had always struggled with her conscience when it came to her work.

"This is a crime," she said.

"It is," Walter agreed.

"This one looks like it might have survived past birth. She's still alive after the brain surgery." Gloria had tears running down her cheek, more out of anger and frustration than sadness.

"I wonder what they do with them," Walter said.

"I don't think I want to know," Gloria answered.

"Have you ever seen any kids around here?"

They stood in silence contemplating the tiny being's possible future that would never be.

"Shall we?" Walter interrupted the silence.

Gloria connected her tablet and Walter reached for the unit's power switch.

Suddenly, Gloria gasped and grabbed Walter's arm.

"What?"

"Look!" She pointed.

The baby had opened its eyes and was studying them with an intense curiosity. Then she smiled.

"Oh my God…" Gloria felt her knees give way.

"Holy shit!"

"Walter, we can't," Gloria said. "It would be murder!"

The baby cocked her head and watched them intently.

It was unnerving.

Walter said nothing.

Gloria waited.

Finally he said: "Ok, assuming she survives the birth, then what?"

Gloria thought for a moment. "This place has formula and diapers. We could hide her in my quarters and smuggle her out when they dismiss us."

"Great plan until she cries," Walter said.

"Good point," Gloria agreed.

There was a long pause while the baby observed them as if she understood the seriousness of the situation.

"I'll have to take off with her," Gloria said.

"Are you nuts? They'll come after you." Walter looked alarmed.

She nodded. "But maybe you can buy me some time."

Walter hesitated. "That I can do," he said.

They agreed to record the powering down of the unit before removing the infant. Gloria downloaded and wiped the data of the specimen. It would take an investigation to discover that the unit had housed another embryo. Next they replaced the baby with a new fetus and fudged the data, so it appeared as if this was the original inhabitant. When the cleaning crew came, all units would be occupied by dead embryos. Gloria held the shivering new born against her chest. Walter handed her a clean blanket in which to wrap the baby. It wasn't crying, but looking into Gloria's face as if studying her.

"How do we get her out of here and into my quarters?" Walter looked around and spotted a dirty linen cart. "Quick! Put her in here."

Gloria lowered the infant into the laundry cart and covered her.

"Let's go!"

Walter opened the door and peered into the corridor. "Looks empty," he said, "follow me."

They rolled the laundry cart along the hallway and around the corner.

"Is the gestation room ready for cleaning?" Jorge looked questioningly at the laundry cart.

Gloria felt her heart skip a beat, but Walter answered, "Yeah sure, go ahead."

Jorge hesitated still looking at the dirty linen cart.

"You better hurry, Jorge. Chief wants it done yesterday." Walter rolled his eyes and cocked his head towards the gestation room.

"Right." Jorge pushed his cart past them and disappeared around the corner.

Walter grabbed Gloria by the arm and steered her forward.

A few minutes later, they stopped in front of Gloria's room. She unlocked her door, quickly bent over the linen cart, picked up the baby, and disappeared into her quarters.

Walter moved on with the cart heading for the dirty laundry chute.

Gloria deposited the baby on her bed and removed a
bottle of formula from her lab coat pocket. The baby
watched her place the bottle into warm water.

There was a knock at the door.

"Gloria, it's Walter!"

Gloria opened the door.

Walter walked over to the bed and took a seat.

"Let's look at you, little stowaway." He picked up the
baby and couldn't help but smile at her. To his
surprised, she smiled back.

"Well, what ya know... that little imp is grinning at
me."

Gloria returned with the bottle, took the baby from
Walter and fed her.

"Now what?" she asked.

"Now we need to get her out of here. Do you have a
small suitcase?"

While Walter prepared a baby bed in the trunk of
Gloria's car, she raced around her room packing
formula, diapers, and a few belongings into an
oversized purse. She didn't dare take a suitcase as this
would appear suspicious.

A short while later they met up in the parking garage.

"Where is she?" Gloria asked.

"Asleep in the trunk. Don't stop until you're well out
of range of the lab. And here... take this." Walter held
up a USB stick.

"What is it?" Gloria asked.

"Leverage."

"Thank you, Walter." She put her arms around his
neck. "Thank you".

14

"You're welcome…" He gave her a tight squeeze.
"Now get going," he said, "and don't get caught!"
She nodded, got in the car and drove away.

The main gate to the compound was closed as
Gloria knew it would be. She slowed the car and
lowered the window.
"Good day, Ma'am," the security guard said bending
down to look into the car.
"Where are you headed?"
"Into town, I need to pick up a few personal care
items." Gloria hoped that alluding to feminine hygiene
products would forestall further questions.
A second guard approached, opened the back door, and
looked around.
"Ma'am, we've been asked to increase security. Please
open your trunk."
Gloria's hands tightened on the wheel. She tried to
think of a way out, but nothing occurred to her.
"Your trunk, Ma'am?"
Gloria pulled the lever that released the trunk latch.
The two guards walked around the car.
Should she try to drive through the closed gate? She
doubted the car would pick up enough speed to crash
the gate. Even if she made it through, she didn't want
to take a chance and hurt the baby. But if she didn't,
the baby would die. She closed her eyes, put the foot
on the gas pedal, and…
"You're good to go, Ma'am." The guard pressed a
remote control, and the gate opened.

Gloria put the car in gear, and with her heart hammering in her throat, she drove away from the lab.

As soon as she was well out of sight, she pulled into a deserted country road and drove until she reached a spot sheltered by trees. There she got out, ran around the car and opened the trunk. It was empty! She couldn't believe Walter had double-crossed her. Where was the child?

Just as she got ready to close the lid, she heard a sound. She stared at the empty trunk and understanding dawned. She lifted the carpet and opened the cover to the spare wheel. Instead of a tire, she found her small suitcase, lined with rolled up towels. Wedged between them, now crying in earnest, was the baby.

"Walter, you're a genius!" She stooped and picked up the child.

Chapter 2

Gloria sat shivering and wet from rain on a bus, hugging the sleeping newborn to her chest to keep her warm. Now and then she used her sleeve to wipe the condensation off the window and cast an anxious glance into the night. Was she being followed? The darkness remained unbroken and the street behind her deserted. She allowed herself to drift off into a restless sleep, but when the baby stirred in her arms, Gloria was instantly alert again. She let her mind return to yesterday.

Gloria had driven to the bank where she had closed her accounts and taken out her assets in cash. Next she had made a trip to Walmart and bought a few essentials for herself and the baby. As hard as it was, she had abandoned her car in the parking lot, called a cab, and carried on by bus. Until she obtained a new identity, she needed to rid herself of anything traceable. Unfortunately, this included both her cell phone and her car. Gloria hoped that she had taken every precaution to delay being found.

The night seemed to go on forever. When dawn broke, the bus reached its destination. Gloria joined the queue of other stiff and yawning passengers as they shuffled along the aisle and climbed out of the bus. She looked around nervously. The bus terminal was an unfriendly and frightening place. She picked up her

small suitcase and followed the other travelers into the building searching for a sign that promised 'Taxi'. Still looking over her shoulder from time to time, Gloria made her way through the bus terminal to the other side where she spotted a row of taxis waiting for potential customers. She stood for a moment uncertain which of the yawning drivers were to get her business. Finally she decided on an elderly black man standing beside his cab holding a steaming cup of coffee. There was something comforting in that scene, so Gloria approached him. He greeted her with a kind smile. "Where can I take you today, Miss?"
"Can you recommend a small hotel or bed and breakfast?" she asked.
The cab was warm and Gloria felt the chill ebb away. She knew they would come looking for her and the baby, but hopefully she had bought them enough time.

The cabbie dropped her off in front of a small motel which gave the impression of loving neglect. The paint was peeling and the lawn uncut, but there were flower urns framing the front entrance. Gloria walked into the reception area and hesitated before ringing the bell. It was very early in the morning. Perhaps the owners were still fast asleep. On the second ring, she heard footsteps and a woman's voice calling, "I'm coming. I'm coming already!" Gloria found herself face to face with an elderly white-haired lady in a pink bathrobe. "Yes?" she inquired.
"I would like to book a room," Gloria said.
"For how many nights?"

Before Gloria had a chance to answer, the baby awoke and began to scream. It was a strange and high-pitched sound. The old lady looked at the baby and back at Gloria.

"Two nights please," Gloria answered.

"I hope she doesn't scream all night." The old lady handed Gloria a key. "Number 22, outside and to your right. Sign here."

Gloria stared at the book for a moment before signing it Holly Miller.

"How will you be paying?"

"Cash," Gloria said.

"I give discount for cash... and I ask no questions."

Room number 22 was shabby but clean. Gloria gently put the baby on the bed and the suitcase on the floor.

"Let's look after you, little one," she said.

The baby stopped crying and smiled at her.

Over the next two weeks, Gloria traveled from one town to the next staying in various motels under different names. When she was not tending to the baby, she was on her laptop analyzing the data Walter had given her. It became clear that she was in deep trouble. She didn't know why the previous government had gone to such length trying to create human GMOs. During the past three years she and Walter had grown twenty infants to full gestation. Of those twenty, twelve had survived past the first month and been shipped elsewhere. The data on the USB stick was painting a frightening picture. Gloria didn't know how

Walter had obtained it, but she understood why he had given it to her.

Every night, Gloria sat on her bed cuddling with the baby and watching the news in tense anticipation. So far, there was nothing on her disappearance.

It seemed to Gloria as if the baby could sense the importance of this nightly ritual.

Even if she had been fussy only moments earlier, the minute she heard the news anchor speak, she became quiet and watched the television.

"Good evening, Ladies and Gentlemen! On the news tonight: Police have filed a missing person report for this woman."

Gloria's heart skipped a beat. The TV screen had filled with a picture of her.

"Gloria Walker went missing from her home two weeks ago. It is believed that she kidnapped her infant daughter shortly after birth. The baby has a rare condition and requires medical attention. The public is advised not to approach Ms. Walker directly as she is considered unstable. Please call...."

Gloria turned off the TV and sat in stunned silence. Over the past two weeks, she had stayed in five different motels under five different names. She had even cut and colored her hair as an added precaution. At times, she had told herself she was being paranoid, that no one was coming after her. This newscast finally made it real. They were looking for her. She felt chills running up her spine. It was time to put the next phase of her plan into action.

Two years ago the U.S. had followed the lead of countries like Germany and Japan to install baby bins in all major cities, despite criticism that the bins allowed mothers to stay anonymous and deprive children of the right to know their parentage. The bins had already saved the lives of countless newborns whose desperate mothers might have abandoned them elsewhere if the bins didn't exist.

Gloria stood in the darkness looking up and down the deserted street. Once she opened the hatch, there was no turning back. The baby whimpered. Gloria looked at the earnest little face.

"Sweetheart, if there was any other way, I wouldn't leave you." Tears were burning her eyes. She hadn't anticipated forming such a strong attachment to the infant. "I'm trying to save your life. Please believe me," she pleaded.

The baby's lower lip quivered.

Gloria reached for the hatch and pulled it open. Inside was a cozy, heated bed which contained paperwork that allowed the mother to leave some information. Gloria hesitated. She had spent many hours trying to figure out a message for the child. Information she could decipher when she was older. Gloria kissed the baby's tiny forehead and gently lifted her into the bed. Then she pulled an envelope from her pocket and placed it on top of the baby. The baby lay very still looking up at Gloria. Once the bin was closed, it could not be reopened.

"I'm sorry." Gloria closed her eyes and shut the hatch.

"Goodbye, little one," she whispered and walked away.

Inside the dark hatch, a little voice answered: "Bye".

When the alarm went off at Safe Haven Julie got up to answer it.

"We have a little customer," she called out to her colleague.

Andrea joined her at the hatch. Julie opened the inside door, and the bed slid towards them. They stared in surprise. As staff of a baby abandonment center, they had seen their share of deformities. Julie picked up the envelope and handed it to Andrea. It was sealed and addressed to 'Gemah'.

Andrea added it to a new folder and marked the name and time on the intake form. 3:25 a.m. - no surprise there. Most infants were abandoned under the cover of darkness.

Julie carried the child over to the examination room and undressed her for a medical exam.

"The infant is female," she dictated to Andrea whose job it was to take notes.

"She appears to be in good physical health," Julie continued as she picked up the baby and examined her back.

"Wait," she said and bent down for a closer look.

"She's got an odd birthmark or scar at the back of her neck." Andrea picked up a camera and took a picture. Julie placed the baby on her back and removed the small hat that covered most of the oversized head. She gasped.

"She's got no ears!"

Instead of cartilage and earlobes, there was a small hole in each side of the head.

"Look here." Julie pointed at the top of the baby's head. "Is that a scar? Maybe she had surgery."

"Do you think she's deaf?" Andrea asked.

Julie walked around the examination table to stand behind the baby. She clapped her hands as loud as she could. The baby startled and began to scream. Andrea and Julie looked at each other. It was like no sound they had ever heard a baby make.

"It's ok," Andrea said soothingly.

"She's not deaf," Julie remarked.

She picked up the Otoscope and checked the ear holes. "Seems ok," she said and proceeded to shine the light into the baby's eyes. It was reflected back at her.

Julie looked at Andrea. "This is no normal baby!"

"And that's probably why she's here and not with her mother," Andrea answered taking a picture of the baby's head while Julie picked up a stethoscope.

"This is going to be a bit cold." Julie breathed on the flat end of the instrument trying to warm it up before placing it on the baby's chest.

"Normal," she announced a short while later, "150 beats per minute".

Next, she took the baby's legs and pressed them apart. "Hips appear normal," she said and proceeded to check knees and feet.

"What's this?" Andrea bent down to take a closer look.

"She's got webbed toes," Julie said in surprise. Andrea took a picture and made a note in the chart.

23

"How would you describe her skin?" Julie asked.

"Grey and…" Andrea hesitated. "Rubbery?"

"Yeah, I know. It's weird," Julie answered.

"Do you want to bathe her or shall I?" Andrea asked.

"I'll do it." Julie carried the baby over to the basin.

Andrea went back to her desk to type the intake form. A short while later she heard Julie call for help. Andrea abandoned her computer and rushed into the examination room. Julie stood helplessly by the sink.

"I can't hold on to her. She squirms like a fish!"

Sure enough, there was water splashing everywhere as the baby kicked and dove with her head under water. Andrea plunged both hands into the tub and grasped the baby firmly around the middle.

"My God, she's strong!"

Andrea lifted her up into the towel that Julie was holding in anticipation.

"Gotcha!" she said wrapping up the baby which was screaming in frustration.

Andrea laughed. "She sure likes the water."

"Uh-huh," Julie said less enthusiastically. "I'm soaked."

A short while later Andrea and Julie sat together with a coffee. The baby had been fed and was now fast asleep.

"Let's see what the letter says." Julie opened the envelope and withdrew a piece of paper. She unfolded it, stared at it for a moment and then passed it to Andrea who read,

"Dear Gemah, I hope you like it."

This sentence was followed by several lines of handwritten sheet music.

Chapter 3

"Happy birthday, dear Gemah, happy birthday to you!" The out of tune chorus sang at the top of their lungs. Gemah grimaced as the noise assaulted her ears. "Ok Sweetheart, go ahead and blow out your candles." Gemah's mother said placing a splendid birthday cake in front of her. Gemah took a deep breath, but before she had the chance to blow out the candles, her father warned, "Careful now, Gem! You don't want to blow up the entire cake again like last year."

Gemah exhaled and rolled her eyes. "Thanks for reminding me, Dad!" She took another breath and gently blew out all twelve candles.

"Lungs like a whale!" her Dad teased.

After everyone had their fill of cake, it was time to open presents.

"Mine first! Mine first!" an excited little girl shouted handing Gemah a large box.

"Hmm...," Gemah stared hard at the gift for a moment then said, "It's a charm bracelet."

She removed the wrapping and opened the box. Inside was another box, this one wrapped in tin foil. Inside this box, was another wrapped in paper towel, followed by an even smaller box filled with toilet paper, and finally a tiny case which contained a charm bracelet. Everyone clapped and cheered.

"Mine next!" another girl picked up an even bigger box and handed it to Gemah. Again, Gemah paused for a moment staring hard at the gift before she announced,

"It's a new set of pencil crayons." This box also contained several smaller boxes covered in bubble wrap.

After Gemah had guessed and unwrapped all her gifts, the living room was littered with boxes, bubble wrap, tin foil, paper towel, toilet paper, Styrofoam, and gift wrap. Everyone had tried their best to outsmart Gemah's ability of seeing inside a wrapped birthday present. Over the years, the boxes had become larger and the wrapping jobs more elaborate, but to no avail. Gemah's mysterious x-ray vision could penetrate whatever wrapping material her friends could think of.

Gemah didn't always have friends. Her strange appearance and high-pitched voice made her an easy target for teasing. It wasn't until she had displayed some of her unique talents, like seeing into closed objects, that she had gained in popularity.

After everyone had left and the living room was restored to its former order, Gemah kissed her parents good night, "Mom, can you come upstairs and tug me in?"

"Aren't you getting a bit too old for that?" her Dad asked.

"Of course I'll tug you in," Nancy answered.

A short while later, her mother sat down on Gemah's bed.

"Mom, tell me again the story of how you found me," Gemah asked.

"You've heard it a thousand times." Nancy laughed.

"Please," Gemah pleaded.

"Fine," her mother agreed. "Dad and I had decided to adopt a baby and were on a waiting list. One day, we got a phone call telling us that a special little girl was looking for a new home. I think it was the way you looked at me the first time I held you. As if you understood our conversation. Then you gave me a big smile, and it just melted my heart. I said 'hi there' and to my surprise you said 'hi' back. You shouldn't have been able to talk yet. The doctor figured you were only about a month old. That's when I knew you must be a very special baby."

Nancy smiled and pulled the blanket up a little higher.

"Good night, Darling."

"Good night, Mom."

When Gemah came downstairs for breakfast the next day, she was surprised to find her father sitting at the breakfast table.

"How come you're not at work, Dad?" she asked.

"Oh, I'm going in later today," Bill said and buried his head in the morning paper. He was one of those individuals who preferred reading the paper instead of surfing the web.

Gemah looked at the clock.

"Mom, we're late for school. You didn't wake me."

"Yes, I know, Dear," Nancy answered without offering further explanation.

As soon as Gemah had eaten breakfast, Bill said, "Are we ready to go?"

"Everything's packed," Nancy answered with a cryptic smile.

"What's going on?" Gemah asked.

"Never you mind, Gem. Got your school bag?" Without waiting for a reply, Bill headed for the front door.

"You're both taking me to school today?" Gemah asked when her parents climbed into the car.

"Let's go," her father said cheerfully.

By the time they arrived at the school, they were half an hour late.

"What am I going to tell my teacher?" Gemah asked.

"Hmm... I don't know," Bill said, looking at Nancy.

"What if we don't bother with school today and just keep driving?" she answered.

"Good idea!" Bill put the car in gear.

"Where shall we go?" he asked.

Gemah's mother rummaged in her purse and held up three tickets. "How about a trip to Discovery Cove?"

Gemah let out a squeal of delight. "OMG you guys are amazing! You had this planned all along! You fooled me!"

Her parents laughed. "It's hard to fool you. But yes, we did!"

Discovery Cove was a lush man made park of rocky lagoons, winding rivers and tropical vegetation. It was hard to decide what to do first: visit the waterfalls, feed the tropical birds or swim with the dolphins.

"The dolphins!" Gemah jumped with excitement.

"Ok, the dolphins first," her father agreed.

Gemah could hear the dolphins long before she could see them. Her sensitive ears picked up the clicks and whistles over the hum of people talking and laughing. Her heartbeat quickened. There was something familiar about those sounds. She started to run.

"Wait!" her parents shouted after her, but Gemah couldn't help herself. She ran towards the sounds of the dolphins as fast as her legs would carry her.

When she rounded a bend in the road, she saw a large lagoon where four Bottlenose Dolphins were jumping in a graceful arc above the water.

Gemah stopped for a moment to catch her breath before walking up to the water.

"Dolphins may be more intelligent than humans," the trainer said. "Research suggests that they can convey and receive twenty times the information we can. They can even project images to each other. A dolphin can recognize itself in a mirror, follow a recipe and engage in cognitive thinking. Each dolphin invents a signature whistle which is used as identification by other dolphins much like humans use names."

Gemah stood at the small fence that separated the public from the water. To her surprise, she felt the scar on the back of her neck contract and expand. Without conscious thought, she gave a shrill whistle. Four dolphin heads turned as one. The sleek bodies shot through the water towards her. The trainer blew her whistle to no avail. Gemah climbed up to the top rung of the fence and leaned over the water. The dolphins reared up in front of her whistling. She

31

whistled back. The public became aware of the exchange. Cell phones and cameras pointed at Gemah. The trainer left her place at the pool. Whistle forgotten, she ran yelling at Gemah to get down. Gemah was unaware of her surroundings. She focused entirely on her conversation with the dolphins. Suddenly she lost her footing and fell head first into the pool.

Just at that moment, her parents came into view. "Gemah!" her mother screamed.

Gemah's head disappeared below the water. The trainer was on her cell phone calling for help. People rushed the fence for a better look. The girl's baseball cap floated on the water's surface which had gone eerily still. The dolphins had taken Gemah to the bottom of the pool. The trainer handed her whistle and phone to a stranger, climbed the fence and jumped. With strong strokes she swam towards the middle of the lagoon. The minutes trickled by. The crowd became quiet as if people were collectively holding their breath.

A golf cart appeared and park personnel jumped out and ran towards the pool. Suddenly there was a new commotion. A man yelled: "Nancy!"

A woman lay crumpled on the ground.

"Help!" Bill shouted. "My wife!" He shook her shoulders in desperation. The park personnel ran towards Bill. Just as an ambulance pulled up, there was a loud splash. The dolphins accompanied by Gemah broke the surface. They jumped as one and disappeared again. The crowd gasped. Phones and cameras pointed at the pool, their owners hoping to catch a replay.

Gemah's head appeared again. She swam towards the side of the pool accompanied by dolphins on either side. Even though the trainer was a strong swimmer, she had no chance of keeping up. Gemah arrived at the water's edge within seconds and turned to the dolphins. There was a short conversation of quiet clicks and whistles. Gemah gently touched each dolphin before she pulled herself out of the water with one swift and powerful movement.

Gemah sat next to her father in a hospital lounge. Even though she had changed into dry clothing, she was shivering from shock. A nurse wrapped her in a warm blanket.

Gemah wanted to say she was sorry, but the words wouldn't come. They sat in silence, each alone with their thoughts and fears.

Finally, the door opened, and a middle-aged doctor entered.

"Mr Mitchell?"

"Yes?"

The doctor pulled up a chair and sat down in front of Gemah and her father. His face was grave. "Your wife suffered a massive brain aneurism. We tried to relieve the pressure, but the damage was too great…"

Bill stared at him. "She's…?"

"Yes. She's gone. I'm sorry for your loss."

Bill said nothing. He stared at the doctor trying to comprehend the magnitude of his loss. The doctor waited patiently for questions.

Gemah stood up. "My mother is dead?"

The doctor looked at her and nodded. He took in the strange appearance of the child in front of him, her oversized bald head, lack of facial hair, missing ears, and gray tinged skin. When she spoke, he noticed that her front teeth were sharp pegs and her voice had a high-pitched quality. She had virtually no neck and her head was propped on top of a powerful, squat body. She was the ugliest child he had ever seen.

"Would you like to see her and say your goodbyes?" he asked.

Bill nodded, still unable to speak. They followed the doctor out of the lounge and down the hall. He stopped in front of a room and pushed open the door. "Take as long as you like. I'll be at the nursing station if you need me."

Bill and Gemah hesitated before entering the room. Nancy lay on a bed, her head heavily bandaged. They approached, each taking one side. Gemah reached for her mother's hand. It was cool, and no longer felt right. She wished she could cry, but her eyes stayed dry. She whimpered.

Bill sat on a chair beside the bed. He couldn't take his eyes off Nancy. After some time, he leaned forward, rested his head on his dead wife's chest and wept.

The next weeks were a blur to Gemah. Her father explained that the autopsy had revealed a weakness in Nancy's artery which had given way under pressure of physical exertion.

"The doctor said, it could have happened at any time. It was inevitable."

"But if I hadn't run… if I hadn't fallen into the water…"

"It wasn't your fault, Gem!"

No matter what her father said, Gemah couldn't help but think she was to blame for her mother's death. Her guilt feelings and grief weren't her only problems. More than one visitor at Discovery Cove had managed to get film footage of her. The video of the strange girl talking to dolphins had gone viral. She had become an unwilling celebrity. Kids at school gawked even more than usual, strangers approached her in the street, and one day she came home to find reporters assembled in front of the house.

Finally her father said, "Gem, I've been thinking… your mother left us a sizable life insurance, enough for you to attend a really good private school."

"But… You want to send me away?"

"I think it's for the best."

"But Dad! What about my friends? What about you?"

"Gem, I can't look after you anymore. I've got to get my life in order. I can't raise you on my own…"

Gemah stood rooted to the floor. Her pain and disbelief ran so deep, she had no words.

"You're sending me away because I killed Mom!"

"That's not true."

Gemah stared at her grief stricken father. Suddenly the family photograph above the fireplace shattered. She turned and ran upstairs to her room.

"Gem! Gemah!"

Chapter 4

The school her father had picked was an institution geared towards gifted children. Gemah considered failing the admission exam, but what was the point? Her father was determined to send her away. He would probably find another school. The thought of starting a new life grew on Gemah. Since her mother's death, the house no longer felt like home. Perhaps going away would help with the emptiness inside and the pressure in her chest.

Two weeks later Gemah and her father were on their way to the Cerebral Institute For The Highly Gifted. The building, an imposing four story structure of sandstone and brick, had many dormers and mullion windows. As they drove up the laneway, Gemah marveled at the beauty of the grounds. Lush green grass stretched out in front of the building framed by mature oak and maple trees.

Standing under the big entrance arch, Gemah felt dwarfed as she waited for the large double doors to open. When they did, she found herself in front of a short, plump woman wearing an apron.

"Come in," she invited with a jolly voice, "You must be Gemah. We've been waiting for you." They stepped inside and Gemah looked around in wonder. They stood in a large wood paneled foyer with a big center stairway splitting at the top and leading to the next floor. Framed photographs of former directors, staff and students decorated the walls.

"I'm the housekeeper, Mrs. Phillips," the older woman introduced herself. "Leave your luggage here and I will have it brought to your dorm. Now follow me and I'll introduce you to our director, Dr. Barnes."

They trailed Mrs. Phillips and stood behind her as she knocked on a closed door. They entered a small office where a secretary was busy at work. She looked up and said: "Dr. Barnes expecting you. Go right ahead."

Mrs. Phillips knocked on yet another door and soon they were face to face with Dr. Barnes, an older and distinguished gentleman. As soon as they entered, he rose from behind a big wooden desk and shook Gemah's and Bill's hands. "I'm glad you're here, Gemah. Please sit down."

"There must be something very special about you. We've never had a student receive a perfect score on our admission exam. We thought it impossible... until now."

"Mr. Mitchell," Barnes turned to address Bill. "We estimate your daughter's IQ to be well above 200." When Bill looked confused, he added. "For reference, Einstein's IQ was between 160 and 190". Bill stared at Gemah who was biting her lip.

"Gemah," Dr. Barnes said, "Can you tell me what's on your mind at this moment?"

Caught off guard, Gemah answered: "I-I remembered an article I read on solar storms raining large electrically charged particles on Earth's atmosphere depleting the upper level ozone for weeks and even months." Gemah looked around into the stunned silence, before continuing: "I was also contemplating that certain aspects of Einstein's theory contain serious philosophical and logical inconsistencies which nullify it as a basis for dynamic considerations, however, I have yet to come to a permanent conclusion on this." Bill looked at his daughter. "Gemah... I had no idea..."

Gemah stared down at her clasped hands. "Dad... I didn't want to appear even weirder than the other kids already thought I was."

Before Bill could answer, Barnes said: "Gemah, here at the Cerebral Institute for the Highly Gifted, all the students are very intelligent and most found that they didn't fit in at their regular schools. You don't have to hide your intelligence here. You're in good company." Gemah looked up and smiled at him.

"And now, Mrs. Phillips will get you acquainted with the house rules and show you around. Welcome to CIHG."

The first few days were hard for Gemah. Despite Dr. Barnes' assurance that she belonged at CIHG, she found that her appearance made her an outsider. The other students weren't physically assaulting her as had happened in the past, but they were giving her a wide berth. Nobody wanted to be associated with 'the Weirdo'. The only girl talking to her was her roommate Sarah. Her social awkwardness made her as much an outsider as Gemah. As they were roommates, they formed an unspoken kinship, spending most of their free time in their room rather than in the library or student lounge. At night under the cover of darkness, they shared confidences about their families and the events that had shaped their lives. When this topic was exhausted, Sarah suggested they play a game of 'guess the number'.

"I think of a number between one and ten, and you have to guess it."

"Ok," Gemah agreed. "You go first."

"Got it, start guessing." Sarah said.

"Three."

"Right! Your turn."

"Ok, go ahead." Gemah said forming a big nine in her head and sending it across the room to Sarah.

"Six," Sarah said.

"Nope, guess again."

"Hmm... Five?"

"No… it was nine."

"Darn… ok, your turn again."

When Gemah had guessed ten out of ten numbers correctly while Sarah had managed only three, Sarah said: "You freak me out. I don't think I want to play this game with you anymore."

"It was just luck," Gemah said, but deep inside she knew it must have been more than that. If she could 'see' inside her birthday presents and guess all ten numbers correctly, what else could she do?

Chapter 5

Bill sat with a glass of Whiskey in his favorite armchair reading a crime thriller. He should be in bed sleeping, but he had read himself awake. It was much easier to sit up with a good book and Whiskey than to be alone with his thoughts in an empty bed.

He put the book down. Perhaps he should sell the house. It was far too big and empty without Nancy and Gemah. He poured himself another glass and drank feeling the alcohol go to his head. He reached for his book, but halted in mid air. Was there a noise? He sat up and listened but heard nothing. Maybe he had imagined it.

Bill picked up the book again but found he re-read the same paragraph. He was still listening. There it was again – a quiet scraping sound. He got up and swayed on the spot.   The scraping noise stopped. He must have read too many crime dramas or watched too many thrillers. A cold shiver ran up his spine. He reached for the lamp and extinguished it. Should he call 911? What if all he'd heard was a mouse? He would feel rather stupid. He waited holding his breath. The scraping noise started again. As quietly as he could, Bill crept across the living room and into the kitchen. The sound came from the back door. He peered around the corner. There, almost indistinguishable from the darkness, was a black shadow. Bill turned and ran to the phone. He picked up the receiver and listened for a dial tone – silence.

This was exactly like one of his crime thrillers. He hurried towards the bedroom where his cell phone was charging. Before he could reach it, the intruder had cut through the glass and entered the kitchen. Bill armed himself with a heavy candlestick and ran into the bathroom locking the door.

"Mr. Mitchell," a man's voice said. "We know you're in there. Come out with your hands above your head."

Bill stood rooted to the floor. His thoughts were racing. The intruder knew his name. Wasn't this unusual for a regular break and enter?

"Mr. Mitchell, this is your final chance. Unlock the door or we'll open fire!"

Bill looked around the bathroom. The window wasn't large enough to escape. The best option was to seek shelter. He jumped into the bathtub just as the door crashed open. Two men, masked and dressed in black, hauled him to his feet. One stood Bill up against the wall and pointed a gun in his face.

"Search the house," he instructed the second man.

"Who are you?" Bill asked.

"Keep quiet and cooperate! You don't want to get hurt."

"She's not here." The second man reported a few minutes later.

"Where is your daughter, Mr. Mitchell?" The man tightened his grip on Bill's collar.

"What do you want with Gemah?"

"Answer me!" The man shook Bill roughly.

Bill said nothing.
The man pulled back his fist and drove it hard into
Bill's face.
"Where is Gemah?"
Bill spat out blood his head spinning with alcohol and
pain. The assailant punched him into the stomach. Bill
doubled over and coughed. His eyes found the
candlestick still grasped tightly in his right hand. This
discovery gave him new hope. Bill came up coughing
and brought the candlestick down on his opponent's
head. His assailant grunted and released his grip. The
second man sprang forward. He aimed a blow at Bill
who dodged it. Before Bill could retaliate, the first man
had recovered. He pushed Bill hard in the chest. Bill
lost his balance and went over backwards. The men
sprang forward to catch him, but missed. Bill fell
hitting his neck on the edge of the tub. His body went
limp. The first man crouched down and put his fingers
to Bill's throat feeling for a pulse.
He turned to look at his partner and shook his head.
"Broken neck," he said. "Search the house for the
girl's whereabouts… and make it look like a common
burglary."
"Yes, Sir!"

Chapter 6

There was a knock at the classroom door. It was Mrs. Phillips.

"I have come to collect Gemah. Dr. Barnes wishes to see her."

"Can't it wait? We're in the middle of a test."

"No, it's urgent." Mrs. Phillip stepped past the teacher and walked over to Gemah.

"Please bring your belongings and follow me." Everyone stared at Gemah as she abandoned her test and packed her bag. What had she done? Was she being expelled? She gave her teacher an uncertain look. He shrugged and returned a reassuring smile.

As Gemah followed Mrs. Phillips, she stared hard at the back of her head. If she could read Sarah's numbers, perhaps she could glimpse Mrs. Phillips' thoughts. She saw an image of police officers and Dr. Barnes, before she was overwhelmed with emotional upset. This avalanche of feelings made her dizzy. She realized that she had not only seen Mrs. Phillips' thoughts but also tapped into her emotions.

When they entered Dr. Barnes' office, Gemah was not surprised to find him in the company of the two police officers she had seen in Mrs. Phillips' mind.

"Please sit down, Gemah." Dr. Barnes said kindly. Gemah hesitated. Everyone was standing. She felt uncomfortable.

"Gemah," Dr. Barnes began, "I'm afraid I have terrible news." Gemah looked up, but before he could continue, she saw the truth in his mind.

"There was a break-in at your home... and... your father was killed."

He waited to give Gemah time to digest the news. Everything inside her went cold.

"These gentlemen," Dr. Barnes said pointing at the officers, "have a few questions for you."

"Gemah, I'm Officer Taylor and this is Detective Wilkins. We're very sorry for your loss. We want to apprehend those responsible, but we need your help. Do you know anyone who would have wanted to harm your Dad?"

Gemah shook her head. She felt numb.

"Someone at work, or a neighbor he didn't get along with?"

Gemah shook her head again.

"I understand how shocked you must be," said Taylor. "I'll leave my number. If you can think of anything, please call me."

The two officers nodded and left.

"Mrs. Phillips, please show them out." Dr. Barnes said.

Gemah spent the month following her father's death in a haze. She met with her parents' lawyer to discuss funeral arrangements and the sale of the house. Her parents had appointed Nancy's mother as legal guardian, but as she had predeceased her daughter, Gemah became a ward of the State. Since her parents' estate and life insurance were ample enough to cover the tuition, it was decided she should stay at CIHG. Officer Taylor and Detective Wilkins visited a few more times to ask Gemah about her parents' friends, neighbors, and acquaintances. The officers insisted on accompanying Gemah to the funeral. It was obvious they were surveilling the mourners.

After the funeral, Gemah went to her room and sat on the bed. She felt miserable and forlorn. *I'm all alone in the world now*. She opened the drawer of her nightstand and took out a small box. Gemah lifted the lid. Inside was her mother's wedding band. She reached behind her neck and opened the clasp of her necklace. Her father's ring slid off the chain and into her hand. She kissed the ring and then placed it gently beside her mother's. Gemah looked at the two rings lying beside each other. Her heart ached. Slowly she replaced the lid on the box and returned it to the drawer. As she did so, her hand brushed against a piece of paper. She reached in and pulled it out. It was the envelope her birth mother had left her. She removed the page of sheet music and stared at it.

"Your Mom was probably a famous musician travelling the world," Nancy had postulated. "That's why she couldn't keep you."

Gemah had accepted this theory all her life, but now she was beginning to wonder. It explained the sheet music, but not Gemah's strange appearance or her unique abilities. Bill had played the music to Gemah before she could play piano herself. It was never an enticing tune. As a matter of fact, it had no melody at all. If her birth mother had been a musician, wouldn't there be a melody? If it wasn't a song, what purpose did it serve?

Excitement coursed through Gemah. She jumped off the bed, grabbed pen and paper and began the tedious process of translating musical notes into letters of the alphabet. Her first attempt of using middle C as a starting point failed miserably. She needed to find out what note represented the letter 'A'.

Dear Gemah, I hope you like it.

Those were the only words on the paper. Were they a clue? She tried 'D' and 'G', but the result made no sense. She tried 'I', 'H','Y', and 'L', but no luck. She threw the block of paper down in frustration and went to the bathroom where she caught sight of her image in the mirror.

Mirror Image! There was a famous composition by Mozart called 'The Mirror'. What if either the music or the alphabetic result was a mirror image?

She ran back to her bed, turned the page upside down and used her initial to decode the music. The result still looked odd. The first words were 'Amehcsd Rid'.

Dir Dschema? What if that meant 'Dear Gemah'? And then she got it! Phonetic spelling backwards! Brilliant! It wasn't true phonetic spelling either, but once she figured out the pattern, it didn't take long to translate the letter.

Dear Gemah,
Since you're reading this, I assume you're old enough to learn the truth. I was present at your birth and know

what you are. I have answers for you. If you have
special abilities, hide them. Trust no one. I set up an
email address where you can contact me. Talk to no
one!
 Take care, Gloria

Gemah was stunned. *I know what you are…* WHAT
you are, not WHO you are…
What did that mean? *Talk to no one!*
Gemah walked slowly to her desk and sat down in
front of her laptop. She opened her school email and
stared at the blank screen wondering what to write.

Dear Gloria,
I got your message. What am I?
Gemah

She pressed 'send' just as the door opened and Sarah
entered.
"Hi."
"Hi Sarah."
There was an awkward silence. Sarah busied herself in
her corner of the room while Gemah closed the lid on
her laptop.
"Look, Gem. I can't even begin to know how hard
things are for you right now. If there's anything I can
do, please let me know."
Gemah nodded. "Thanks Sarah. I just need some time
alone to work through stuff."
"Yeah, I guess so. I'll leave the room to you as much
as possible."

Chapter 7

Jennifer Parker was shelving books when her phone buzzed. She retrieved and stared at it. Jennifer led a secluded life as the librarian of a small town in the middle of nowhere. It wasn't often that she received a message. She opened the email and read:

Dear Gloria,
I got your message. What am I?
Gemah

The phone in Jennifer's hand shook uncontrollably as she read and re-read the message. She looked around ensuring the library was deserted before locking the door. Then she went to her office, picked up the receiver and dialed.

"John?"

"Yes?"

"It's... Jennifer... Jennifer Parker."

"Ah, yes... Jennifer... What can I do for you?"

"I received an email from... the girl."

"Read it!"

She read the message.

"Did you answer it?" John asked.

"No."

"Good! You can't respond. If her email is hacked, you can kiss your identity as Jennifer Parker goodbye. What's the email address she used?"

"Gemah.Mitchell@CIHG.com."

There was a moment of silence while John typed.

"That's a school email. She's at the Cerebral Institute for the Highly Gifted."

"Do you think they've located her yet?"

John hesitated. "Hard to say, but I'm sure they're looking for her. That chat with the dolphins was like sending up a flare."

"What can we do to protect her?"

"You'll do nothing, Gloria!" John's voice sounded stern. "The FBI has you under protection so you don't share the same fate as Walter. Remember that!"

"Yes, I know." Gloria bit her lip.

There was a pause before John said: "Now that we know where she is, we can send someone undercover to keep an eye on her."

The first few days following her email message, Gemah ran up to her room between classes to check for a reply but found nothing. The email hadn't bounced, so the address was valid. Maybe Gloria no longer checked that account frequently. After all, it had been more than twelve years.

It felt to Gemah as if she'd lost her parents all over again. When she had first deciphered Gloria's message and discovered it had not been left by her birth mother, her disappointment was mitigated by excitement and possibilities. Now in the absence of any communication, Gemah felt a new kind of despair. She kept to herself and spent increasingly more time alone in her room.

Trust no one! Talk to no one! If Gemah had felt separate from her schoolmates before, it was nothing compared to how she felt now.

If you have special abilities, hide them.

Why would Gloria warn her to hide her abilities and not trust anyone? The only logical conclusion was that someone was looking for her because she had special abilities that were somehow useful.

What special abilities did she have?

She could sense people's emotions. She could look inside closed objects. She could sometimes catch a glimpse of images in people's minds. It wasn't true telepathy, but it had come in handy on more than one occasion. She could talk to dolphins.

The realization went through her like a bolt of lightning. The whole world had seen her communicate with dolphins. Maybe the break-in at the house had not been some random act. Maybe somebody was looking for her. In that case, she was in great danger. Someone was willing to commit murder to find her.

If someone was looking for her, then who? And why? Perhaps they thought she had other more valuable abilities than talking to dolphins. What if there were more things she could do that she didn't know about? The only way to find out was to try different things.

Gemah sat down at her desk and put a pencil in front of her. Staring at it as hard as she could, she willed the pencil to move. Nothing happened. Suddenly the door opened and Sarah came in.

"Hi," she looked at Gemah staring at the pencil.

"Are you trying to make it move?" she asked walking over for a closer look.

"No, of course not!"

Unfortunately, the pencil chose this moment to roll off the desk.

"Cool!"

"That wasn't me!" Gemah protested, but Sarah gave her a 'yeah sure' look.

"No really, Sarah. That was just a coincidence. I wasn't trying to move the pencil or anything."

"You did read my mind when we played the numbers game. Maybe you've got some super powers you don't know about. I overheard Barnes saying that you've got the highest IQ in the school."

"Do me a favour and don't start any rumors about me doing telekinesis. You'll land me in trouble."

"Alright," Sarah said reluctantly, "but you have to promise you'll show me if you figure out how to do it."

Gemah rolled her eyes, but she smiled.

"I'm going to dinner. Are you coming?" Sarah asked.

"In a bit. I've got something to finish. I'll be down shortly."

As soon as the door had closed behind Sarah, the pencil floated up off the ground and placed itself neatly on the desk in front of Gemah.

Chapter 8

"Attention! May I have your attention, please!" Dr. Barnes waited for silence in the auditorium. "The month of October has arrived and with it Halloween is just around the corner. As our older students know, it's tradition for CIHG to have a Halloween dance."

Excited whispers broke out.

"This is an opportunity for students to learn the art of ballroom dancing. Therefore, besides your regular schedule, there will be two evenings a week, when you will meet in the gym for dance lessons. Anyone without a partner by the start of the first lesson will be assigned a dance partner."

He was forced to stop speaking at this point and stood smiling until silence was restored.

"Usually our Phys. Ed teacher, Mrs. Cullen, teaches dance. However, she is on temporary leave attending to family matters. We are very pleased to welcome Mr. Chris Wood at our school." Dr. Barnes turned to a row of chairs behind him where the teachers were sitting. A tall, young man stood up and waved at the students. The short applause that followed was interrupted by an outbreak of whispers and giggles from the girls.

Dr. Barnes pretended not to notice as he carried on, "I'm sure you will give Mr. Wood your full cooperation."

"In addition to Mr. Wood," Barnes continued, "We also have a second newcomer to our staff, Miss Susan Walsh." A pretty, blonde woman stood up and smiled at the students. "Miss Walsh will take on the role of student counselor. Any personal or academic difficulties may be discussed with Miss Walsh in private. That's all for today. You may proceed to your classes."

Amidst the sounds of scraping chairs and chattering students, Wood turned to Susan and extended his right hand.

"It's a pleasure to meet you. How's your dancing?"

Susan blushed. "Ok I guess."

"Good! You can help me teach this lot to dance!" Before she could voice her objection, he got up, flashed her a winning smile, and left.

Initially, Susan had no intention of taking Wood up on his offer, but then she decided it would present an opportunity to meet the students and establish a friendly relationship. Furthermore, she was curious about Wood's dance abilities. Cocky bastard!

For the next two days, the teachers found their job harder than usual. Everyone was preoccupied with the upcoming dance lessons and determined to land a partner before the first session.

"Got anyone yet?" Sarah asked Gemah in the lunch lineup the next day.

"Nope. You?" Sarah shook her head.

"Guess we'll take the luck of the draw," Sarah said.

"Wonder what they'll do if they have an uneven number of boys and girls," Gemah wondered aloud.
"Pair the girls with each other," a voice beside them said. They looked up and found Susan Walsh in line behind them.
"Or the boys!" Sarah giggled at the thought of boys dancing together.
"Or the boys." Susan smiled.
Sarah turned back to Gemah and changed the subject. "Hey, have you figured out that Telekinesis thing yet?" Gemah nearly dropped her lunch tray. She glanced at Susan to check if she had overheard and found her looking back at her with raised eyebrows.
"Of course not!" She sounded unconvincing.
Sarah laughed. She obviously enjoyed teasing Gemah. As soon as Susan turned to fill her plate, Gemah stared at her to get a glimpse of her thoughts but was unable to pick up anything. Susan turned and smiled. "See you tonight." She walked off to sit with the other teachers.

The time for the highly anticipated and somewhat dreaded first dance lesson had finally arrived. As noisy students made their way to the gym, Chris stopped Susan in the hallway.
"Ready?" He asked.
"I am," she said coolly, "are you?"
He ignored her icy tone. "What do you think we should teach them first?"
Susan forgot to pretend anger. "Foxtrot or slow Waltz, maybe?"

He nodded in agreement. "Foxtrot it is."

When they entered the gym, they saw students standing in pairs or small groups. It was immediately apparent who had found a partner and who was aimlessly milling about pretending to look for a friend. Gemah and Sarah weren't pretending. They stood off to one corner looking defeated and prepared to meet their fate.

"Alright everyone," Chris shouted over the din. "Anyone with a partner, please stand over against this wall, anyone without, over here." He pointed at the opposite wall.

The crowd split in two with the majority against the single's wall. Chris and Susan split the group into pairs until only Gemah and Sarah remained. Susan suspected the two had repeatedly escaped to the back to avoid being picked.

"No worries," Chris said. "You two can pair up for now and I'll take turns dancing with you later." Susan turned her back to hide a smile at their horrified faces. Chris instructed the pairs to form a large circle around him and Susan before turning to her.

"Shall we?"

He nodded at Mrs. Phillips whose job it was to man the stereo. Susan and Chris began by demonstrating the basic steps. He could tell she was a very good dancer. She gave him a cocky smile as if to say 'Is that all you can do?'

He smiled back and led her into a turn, a forward run, a wheel, and a reverse turn. Students forgotten, the two of them fought a silent battle on the dance floor that ended with a dip for her. Everyone clapped and cheered.

"It'll be awhile before you'll get to that," Chris said giving Susan a charming smile.

"Let's begin. Boys on the outside facing the girls."

He explained the steps and then circled the room with Susan observing and correcting the resulting chaos. When he got to Gemah and Sarah, he asked, "May I?" and without waiting for a response, he took Gemah by the hand and swung her around to face him. He showed her how to assume proper dance position and signaled Mrs. Phillips to start the music.

"Slow, slow, quick, quick!" he called out and started to dance with Gemah who would have liked nothing better than to sink beneath the floor.

"Don't look down at your feet." he instructed, "They know where to go. It's just like walking." He smiled.

"So how long have you been attending CIHG?" he asked.

"Only a few months," Gemah mumbled.

"I guess you must be pretty smart to be attending this school," Chris continued his small talk.

"I guess so," Gemah agreed.

Suddenly she felt a sharp pain in her back. "Ouch!" She stumbled.

"You ok? Did I step on your feet?"

"No, no… I'm fine." She lied.

While Chris was dancing with Gemah, Susan walked over to Sarah.

"May I have this dance, my lady?" She gave a theatrical bow that made Sarah laugh.

Once they were dancing she said, "So you and Gemah are good friends?"

"We're roommates," Sarah said.

"I hear Gemah's had a tough time lately. Other foot." Susan corrected.

"Yes, she lost both her parents." Sarah stumbled over her feet.

"How terrible! I'm sorry to hear that." They danced in silence for a minute.

"Slow, slow, quick, quick," Susan reminded Sarah before continuing. "So what was that about telekinesis the other day?"

"Oh nothing, I was just teasing."

Susan laughed. "Why would you tease Gemah about telekinesis?"

"Because of the other cool stuff she can do."

At this point Sarah stumbled, and they had to stop dancing.

"Like what? Slow, slow, quick, quick." They picked up the beat and began to dance again.

"Like telepathy and ... I'm not sure what to call it, but Gemah can see into closed objects."

Susan stopped dancing. "What do you mean?"

Sarah glanced over at Gemah who looked unhappy dancing with Mr. Wood and suddenly felt uncomfortable. Maybe she shouldn't have said all that stuff. To her intense relief the music came to an end.

"Thanks for dancing with me." She ran over to Gemah before Susan could hold her back. Gemah had just escaped from Chris and was heading for the far corner with the intention of hiding.

"Wait up!" Sarah shouted.

"What's the matter?" Gemah asked as soon as Sarah caught up with her.

"Nothing." Sarah grabbed Gemah by the arm to steer her behind a crowd of students.

"Everyone get back into a circle, girls on the inside, boys on the outside," Chris called.

As soon as everyone was in position, Chris instructed: "Now boys, you move to the next girl on your left. Everyone should end up with a new partner!"

There was a lot of confusion before everyone, willing or not, stood facing a new partner.

"Hi," Gemah said.

"Hi," the boy answered uncomfortably.

When Gemah looked into his face, she didn't need telepathy to know what he was thinking. The words came unbidden into her head. 'Freak' and 'Gross'.

Before they had a chance to assume dance position Gemah said, "I'm sorry. I... have to go to the bathroom."

She turned and fled from the gym.

Chris turned to Susan as they left the gym. "Thanks for your help. I think it was a pretty good start."

"I agree." She nodded.

They walked in silence. Finally Susan said, "You've got Gemah first period tomorrow morning, right?"

"Yes, why?"

"I'd like to see her in my office. I talked to her roommate Sarah, and it seems Gemah has not adjusted well after her parents' death."

Chris stopped walking. "She's lost both parents?"

"Yes, very tragic, really. Her mother died of a brain aneurism and her father during a burglary."

They started walking again. "How long ago was that?"

"This past summer. That's why I'd like to meet with Gemah as soon as possible. Would you be willing to let her miss gym?"

He shrugged. "I guess so."

They had arrived at her room. "This is me." She pointed at the door.

"Thanks again," he said, "and I hope you'll help me out on Thursday."

"We'll see." She smiled and closed the door.

Chris' room was two doors down and across the hall. As soon as he closed the door, he picked up his cell and dialed.

"Garner here. The device has been deployed successfully."

At the same time, Susan was also on her cell. "Agent Hunt speaking. The device is definitely operational. I have an eyewitness account of telepathy and some sort of ability to see into closed objects. Telekinesis is suspected but not confirmed."

"Good," the voice on the other end responded. "When can you move to phase two?"

"Tomorrow morning, if you're standing by."

"Confirmed. We are ready."

Chapter 9

The next morning, Susan caught up with Gemah and Sarah at the breakfast counter.

"Gemah, I spoke to Mr. Wood, and he's agreed to let you come to my office instead of attending your gym class."

"Why?" Gemah asked. She liked gym.

"You've got such a busy schedule with the upcoming exams, it's the only time that won't interfere with your studies. So, I'll see you around nine?"

Gemah nodded and watched Susan leave.

"I wonder what she wants with me?" she said.

"Um… Gemah," Sarah began uncertainly, "last night at dance lesson, I said some stuff to Miss Walsh that maybe I shouldn't have. I'm sorry."

"What kind of stuff?" Gemah asked.

"Like how you can do telepathy and stuff… " Sarah trailed off.

"Oh," Gemah didn't know what to say. She was angry with Sarah but sensed how sorry she was.

"Look, Gem, I'm really sorry. I had no business telling her that stuff."

"It's ok," Gemah let her off the hook. "I'm sure she doesn't want to see me about flying pencils."

Sarah stared at her. "Flying pencils? You can? You did?"

Gemah smiled at her. "Yeah, but PLEASE keep your mouth shut!"

They grinned at each other and both realized that their friendship had grown much stronger.

It was two minutes to nine when Gemah knocked on Susan's door.

"Enter."

She pushed open the door. Susan got up from behind her desk and walked over to a small coffee table with two comfy armchairs.

"Have a seat, Gemah." She said.

Gemah sat and waited expectantly.

"Dr. Barnes tells me you lost your parents recently."

Gemah nodded.

"You must be terribly lost without them." Susan looked concerned.

Gemah nodded again staring at her clasped hands.

"I understand you were adopted," Susan continued. "Have you thought about contacting your birth mother?"

"I don't know where she is."

"Maybe we can find her," Susan suggested.

Gemah shook her head.

"So you have no idea where she might be?"

"No." Gemah looked up with a hint of defiance. She'd much rather be at the gym.

"Ok then." Susan got up and walked over to her desk. She opened a drawer and withdrew something that looked like a TV remote control.

When Gemah didn't oblige her by asking, Susan said, "Do you know what this is?"

Gemah studied the device and saw something inside she didn't expect. Instead of little wires and computer chips, there was a strange glowing and pulsating mass. She sensed Susan's excitement, but was unable to read her thoughts. She hit a mental brick wall.

"Don't even try," Susan said smiling. "I can protect my mind from yours."

Before Gemah could register surprise, Susan pointed the device at her and pushed one of the buttons. Lights exploded behind Gemah's eyes and there was excruciating pain deep inside her brain. Her body began shaking, and she felt like she would be sick at any moment. Susan watched her with a hungry expression. Gemah doubled over and cradled her head in her hands.

Sarah, HELP! She screamed silently… and then everything went black.

Sarah was climbing a rope when her head exploded with pain. In her surprise she let go and landed hard on the mat. Wood came running.

"Are you ok?"

"Gemah!" Sarah gasped for air.

Chris looked at her in confusion. "Gemah what?"

"Gemah," Sarah said again. "She's… in trouble."

Chris stared at Sarah and then pelted from the gym. As he ran past, the door to Dr. Barnes' office opened.

"Mr. Wood, I'd like a word with you."

Chris skidded to a halt.

"I need your help keeping this hallway clear. One of our students has fallen ill and the paramedics are on their way."

"Who is it?" Chris asked even though he thought he knew.

"Gemah Mitchell. She's having an epileptic seizure." Chris was torn between Dr. Barnes' request and the desire to check on Gemah. He stood uncertainly when he heard footsteps running towards him. Two paramedics pushing a gurney came into view.

"Let me show you to the patient", Chris offered and ran ahead to Susan's office.

When he arrived, he found Gemah on the floor, twitching and foaming at the mouth. She appeared to be unconscious. Susan was beside herself.

"I don't know what happened. One minute we were talking and the next she was convulsing."

The paramedics picked up Gemah and strapped her to the stretcher.

"Where are you taking her," Chris asked.

"St. Michael's hospital, about twenty minutes from here."

"I'm coming with you," he said.

"There's no need." Susan stepped forward. "I'll go with her."

"Then we'll both go!" Chris followed the paramedics out the door.

Chris and Susan sat across from each other with Gemah lying between them. As soon as the doors closed, the back of the ambulance was plunged into semi darkness. One paramedic took Gemah's vitals while the other prepared a syringe.

"What are you giving her?" Chris asked.

The paramedic turned to Chris. "This is not for her. It's for you!" He stabbed the needle hard into Chris' arm.

"I told you not to come," he heard Susan say before he blacked out.

Chapter 10

Gemah opened her eyes. The light was painfully bright and her head was throbbing.

"Water," she croaked.

Someone supported her head and held a straw to her lips. She took a sip and sunk back into the pillow.

"Where am I?" She tried to look around. The room didn't feel like a hospital room.

"You're at a top secret research facility," a familiar voice answered.

Gemah looked up into Susan's face and frowned. She tried to remember what had happened, but her brain felt fuzzy. The last thing she could remember was being in Susan's office.

"You're suffering from the aftereffect of the 'Subjugator'. It'll pass," Susan said without compassion. "Consider it a warning of what can happen if you choose not to cooperate. The device not only has the power to inflict pain, it can also kill. So choose wisely." With these words, she left the room.

Maybe I'm dreaming, Gemah thought. That had to be it, but if it was a dream, why did she ache all over? She closed her eyes and tried to remember what had happened. Slowly images and bits of conversation came back to her. She remembered the device Susan had pointed at her. That must be what Susan had called the 'Subjugator'. Gemah didn't like the sound of that.

But how and why did it work on her? There were more questions than answers.

As she became more alert, she took in her surroundings in more detail. There was a large tinted glass mirror at the far wall. Gemah stared at it and saw right through it. On the other side were two people watching her, Susan and an unknown man in a white lab coat.

She strained her ears and heard Susan ask: "When will she be ready to begin testing?"

"Probably in another few hours. Once she can keep some food down, she'll feel better."

Susan nodded and walked away.

Soon after, the door opened and a disembodied arm pushed a tray of food into the room. Gemah entertained the thought of a hunger strike, but the enticing smell of eggs and toast defeated her willpower. As she took the first bite, she remembered her mother's saying "No matter what you're facing Gem, it's easier on a full stomach." *I miss you, Mom!*

"Hey, Buddy! Wake Up!" Chris felt someone slapping his face. "You drunk or on drugs?" the unknown voice asked.

"Probably Barbiturates," Chris mumbled.

"Get up, Buddy. You'll freeze. C'mon!" Someone lifted him under the shoulders and heaved. Chris found his legs and stood swaying on the spot.

His rescuer studied him with concern. "You ok, man?"

"I think so." Chris nodded. "Where am I?"

"At a truck stop outside of Chicago."

"What the hell?"

"C'mon, let's pour some coffee into ya." The man grabbed Chris by the elbow and steered him towards the restaurant.

He was right. Once the hot coffee took effect, Chris was able to think more clearly.

"What happened?" the trucker asked. "Some of your buddies pull a joke on you like in the movies when a guy is about to get married, and the groomsmen get him drunk and drag him off somewhere?"

"Not exactly," Chris said. He searched his pockets. No phone, no wallet.

"Listen, can I borrow your phone for a minute?"

"Sure thing." The truck driver handed over his phone. Chris got up and walked a few feet away.

"John, it's Chris."

"Garner! Where the hell have you been? They've got the girl!"

"Yes, I know. I was drugged and dumped at a truck stop outside of Chicago. Can you come and get me?"

"Hang on, yes, got the coordinates of your cell."

"Ok, I'll wait here for you."

Chris returned the phone to its owner. "Listen, if you give me your email, I can send you some compensation. I really appreciate you hauling me out of the ditch!"

"Sure thing, man." The two shook hands.

Gemah sat still while the man in the white lab coat attached sensors and hooked her up to an EEG machine. Across from her sat Susan with the

Subjugator held demonstrably high, so Gemah was reminded to cooperate.

Once she was hooked up, the man nodded at Susan who said: "I'm sure you have lots of questions, so let me start by explaining that you are the property of the United States government and therefore have as many rights as a police dog."

Here she paused to give Gemah the opportunity for outrage, but Gemah chose not to give her that satisfaction. Susan continued.

"Your name – GEMAH – is actually not a name, but an acronym. It stands for Genetically Engineered Modified Alien Humanoid. You were created to be a super-weapon that the US could deploy in situations where stealth and superior intelligence was required. Therefore, you were engineered using DNA from several species to give you speed, endurance, and enhanced brain and lung performance."

"Dolphin DNA?" Gemah asked.

Susan nodded with a smile. "Very good".

"Why 'Modified Alien Humanoid'?"

"Your brain was implanted with an alien device prior to birth. It's what boosts your brain power to allow for telepathy and the ability to see into objects or through walls. Of course creating such a powerful being, we needed to ensure that we could control it." Susan waved the hated Subjugator playfully in the air. "Luckily, our alien friends left us this little device."

It was a lot to take in. Gemah felt dizzy. All her life she had asked herself why she looked different, why she had special abilities and such a high IQ, only to discover that she was a GMO with an alien device planted in her brain. She wasn't even human. She was a humanoid, a being with no control over her own life. She was the property of the US government to use as they wished.

She felt numb and defeated.

Susan watched her carefully. "There were other human GMOs, but you're the only one left."

"What do you mean?"

"It seems that your unique genetic makeup using dolphin DNA is the only combination that works with the device over the long term. The others developed seizures and died. Of course we've harvested the devices to be re-implanted into new hosts, but we decided to wait until we could get some of your unique genetic material."

Gemah looked down at her arm. She could see a small puncture wound and the faint trace of blood. The callousness with which Susan described the demise of the other GMO children gave Gemah the chills.

"So you're going to clone me," she said.

"Precisely."

"You've got what you needed. You can let me go then."

Susan gave a derisive laugh. "I thought you had an IQ of 200! You are unique, Gemah, and very valuable."

Gemah felt sick.

"If you have no further questions," Susan continued, "It's time to start with some basic tests. Cooperate and you will be rewarded, boycott our efforts and you will be punished."

Testing consisted of Gemah reading the thoughts of someone stationed in another room looking at cue cards with images. She decided to do her best until she could figure out her options.

After two hours, she began to make mistakes.

"You're not concentrating!" Susan said.

"Sorry," Gemah mumbled. "I'm getting tired and thirsty. Can I have a break?"

"Perhaps it's time to call it a day," the doctor said. "She's probably still recovering from the after-effects of the seizure."

"Fine, we'll start again in the morning." Susan stalked from the room.

To Gemah's surprise, the next morning didn't consist of telepathy testing but of physical fitness. A young woman picked her up and took her to a gym.

"My name is Elle. From now on, you'll work out with me every morning. I'll teach you self defense and advanced hand to hand combat maneuvers."

Elle turned out to be a hard taskmaster. By the end of the first session, Gemah had a bloody nose, and a bruised eye. She was given a short rest in her room with a pack of ice before she was picked up again and taken back to the EEG lab. Once she was hooked up to the machine, Susan placed a pencil on the table in front of her and said "Move it!" Gemah stared at the pencil. Nothing happened.

"Do you need persuading?" Susan asked.

"I can't do it!" Gemah said.

"I don't believe you." Susan looked at the doctor.
"What do you think?"
The doctor glanced at the EEG then at Gemah.
"Can I have a word with you in private?" He asked Susan.
The two left the room but obviously forgot Gemah's acute hearing.
"We need leverage," the doctor said.
"What did you have in mind?"
"Repeated use of the Subjugator may lead to brain damage. Can we get our hands on someone she cares about?" he said.
"Hmm... maybe. Let me see what I can do."

That afternoon, Susan made a call to head office. "We need to hack the girl's school email. I want to know who she's been corresponding with. Get me the IP addresses and locations of any email recipients."

Gloria locked the library doors and walked along the sleepy main street. Nine o'clock in the evening and not a soul around. She pushed her hands deeper into the ample pockets of her coat and tugged it around herself. It was a cold, blustery evening, and the chill cut through her. She was looking forward to coming home and lighting a fire.
Maybe I'll even treat myself to a glass of Sherry, she thought. The idea of indulging in a drink by an open fire made her smile and pick up the pace.

Suddenly she felt uneasy. She looked around, but saw nobody. She could have sworn she'd heard footsteps. Gloria continued to walk, listening. Nothing.

Perhaps she was being silly. She crossed the road and turned into a smaller side street. The wind blew her hair forward into her face. She turned her head. There it was! A shadow dodged into an alley between houses and disappeared.

Gloria's heart was hammering in her chest. She felt breathless. Should she run? She couldn't knock on any doors. This street was full of closed businesses. She pulled her phone out of her pocket. If she dialed now, she'd have to slow her pace, but it was her only chance to call for help.

"I'm currently unavailable. Please leave me a message... "

"John, it's Gloria. I'm being followed."

In the short time it took her to call, the unknown stalker closed the gap. Gloria felt a gloved hand press over her mouth. "Quiet! Not a sound or I'll blow your brains out!"

Gloria froze. A car screeched around the corner and stopped beside them. The door opened.

"In!" The man ordered.

She had no choice. As she ducked her head to climb in, she felt a hard blow against her temple. Gloria crumpled into the backseat.

"I trust you know who this is?" Susan asked. Gemah looked through the two-way mirror into a small room where a woman sat tied to a chair. Her head hung forward and her blonde, messy hair obscured her face.

"No, I don't," Gemah said.

"Go wake her up," Susan said to the doctor.

They watched as he entered the room and gave the woman a rough shake. Her head rolled around, and she moaned. Gemah felt sorry for her.

"She needs a drink of water," she said.

Susan raised her eyebrow at Gemah then spoke into the mike. "Dr. Leung, please get some water for our guest."

The drink appeared to revive Gloria. She was able to lift her head and look around. As soon as Gemah saw her face, she knew who it was. Images of their short time together flooded her brain. This woman had shown her love and compassion. She had risked her own life to save Gemah. Her heart sank. This was the leverage they had discussed. They would use Gloria to blackmail Gemah.

"If I cooperate, will you let her go?" Gemah asked.

Susan smiled at her. "We'll see."

Gemah was once again seated at the table with a pencil in front of her. Across from her sat Gloria looking disheveled. She had a large bruise on her left cheek.

"Now then," Susan said. "Let's see you move that pencil."

"I can't," Gemah answered.

The doctor's hand connected hard with Gloria's face and her head snapped back.

"NO!" Gemah screamed.

"Please," she pleaded. "Please don't hurt her!"

"That's entirely up to you, Gemah," Susan said. "Move the pencil."

Gloria's eyes met Gemah's. They both understood that if Gemah gave in, there would be no end to the blackmail.

Gemah hung her head. "I'm sorry. I can't."

The doctor pulled back a fist ready to strike again. Gloria cringed in anticipation. Gemah concentrated with all her might. The doctor punched, but his hand didn't strike Gloria. An invisible barrier had formed around her. When his fist connected with it, he was thrown backwards and landed in a heap on the floor cradling a bloody hand. Susan was ready with the Subjugator. She pushed a button and Gemah's head exploded in pain.

Gemah awoke to someone gently placing a cool washcloth on her forehead. She tried to open her eyes, but shut them again when a wave of nausea hit her. She moaned.

"Take your time," Gloria said.

Gemah blinked in surprise.

"Here, let me dim the lights."

Once the room was not so bright, Gemah was able to open her eyes.

"Hi." Gloria smiled.

"Hi."

There was an awkward pause,

"You've grown a bit since the last time I saw you," Gloria said.

Gemah struggled to sit up. "They're watching us," She warned.

"I know."

"Why are they letting us stay together?" Gemah asked.
"So they can spy on us, I suspect."
They fell silent. There was so much Gemah wanted to ask, but she didn't dare.

The hours trickled by. They took turns pacing the room and attempting to communicate with looks. With all the telepathy testing, Gemah had become much more receptive. She had no difficulty reading Gloria's thoughts. She wondered if she could plant a thought in return. The next time Gloria looked up, Gemah stared at her
I'm hungry!
Gloria smiled. *Me too!*
It was very rudimentary, but it was a start. Gemah nodded.
She got up and walked over to Gloria making sure her back was to the mirror shielding them from view. Gemah put a finger to her lips in warning. She reached out and touched Gloria's bruised face. Gemah closed her eyes and concentrated. She knew it had worked even before she opened her eyes. Gloria stared in shock.
You healed my bruise?
Gemah nodded and smiled. Gloria reached for Gemah's hand and squeezed it.

By the next morning, both Gemah and Gloria were starving. Elle entered with a breakfast tray and put it in front of Gemah. Then she sat down and waited for Gemah to eat.
"Where's Gloria's breakfast?" Gemah asked.

"Gloria is being punished for your behavior yesterday. You need to eat so we can continue your training. Gloria on the other hand…" she didn't finish.

"Go ahead," Gloria said. "Eat."

"But–," Gemah protested.

"Eat! I'll be fine," Gloria walked into the bathroom.

"And what if I don't?" Gemah said feeling mutinous.

"Susan is standing by with the Subjugator."

"Eat!" Gloria yelled from the bathroom.

Gemah sighed and picked up the fork.

Over the next few days the situation became desperate. Gemah obediently levitated pencils, chairs, desks, and other objects in the hope that Gloria would receive a meal. Their captors had changed tactics and now kept them apart. They only saw each other during Gemah's training sessions, which Gloria attended tied to a chair. It was obvious to Gemah that she was becoming weaker.

Finally Gemah said, "I'm not going to do anything more until you give Gloria some food!"

Susan raised an eyebrow and looked from Gemah to the Subjugator. Gemah tried to use her mental powers to knock the Subjugator out of Susan's hand, but it was protected by a force field.

"Fine! Use that stupid thing on me then! See if I care!"

"No!" Gloria screamed.

Susan stood up. "Remember what I told you," she said. "The device can also kill!" She pushed a button and Gemah collapsed.

Chapter 11

Gloria awoke to the sounds of shouting. She pulled back the covers and climbed out of bed. She was weak. Walking to the door was an effort. She put her ear against it. Something was happening outside. She'd give anything right now to have Gemah's x-ray vision. The voices were getting closer.

She could make out the unmistakable sounds of a fight. She hesitated before pounding on the door and yelling: "In here! I'm in here!"
The fight was approaching. She heard sounds of punches and grunts, then only silence. She felt too weak to continue her shouting. Her legs gave out, and she collapsed in a heap by the door. "In here!" It was barely more than a whisper. Was it enough?

Suddenly the door knob burst and flew across the room leaving a dent in the opposite wall. Gloria had just enough time to roll out of the way before the door opened. A dark figure entered and looked around. "Can you stand?" The man helped Gloria up. She was shivering uncontrollably.
"Here, sit down on the bed. I'll come back for you." When she clung to his hand, he gently pulled it away. "I promise." He ran from the room.

Chris continued along the hallway keeping his back to the wall and his gun in front of him. Every sense was alert. He listened into the darkness. He rounded a corner, then another. All of a sudden, a door opened behind him and someone hurtled through it. Elle flew through the air and planted both feet into his back. She recovered with a somersault. Chris fell forward. Before he could regain his footing, Elle attacked again and knocked the gun out of his hand. It spun down the hall and out of sight. He rolled over on the floor and missed her kick by inches. Chris jumped up in time for her next assault. He was ready for her and blocked her punch. The force threw her back against the wall. Elle screamed in frustration and hurtled forward. He stepped aside, and she missed. Chris used that split second to deliver a karate chop to her right shoulder. She sank to her knees but recovered. Elle launched herself forward and grabbed him around the knees. He lost his balance, and they both fell. It knocked the wind out of him. Elle sat astride and punched his face as hard as she could. His head snapped sideways and hit the wall.

Gemah awoke to the sound of a click by her head and Susan's voice. "I've got a gun pointed at your head, Gemah. Get up and do exactly as I tell you." Gemah sat up, but her last encounter with the Subjugator left her head swimming. She groaned. "Cut the dramatics and get dressed." Gemah did as she was told trying to make sense of the situation. Something wasn't right. "What's going on?" she asked. "You're coming on a trip with me," Susan replied.

The doctor rushed into the room. "They've made it past the guards and into the compound! We have very little time!"

"Thank you, Leung." Susan pointed the gun at him and shot him point blank in the chest.

Gemah screamed.

"Let's go!" Susan said waving the gun in the direction of the door. She had almost reached it when Gloria stumbled into the room.

Gloria threw herself against Susan knocking her off balance. Gemah used the diversion to take the gun out of Susan's hand. It flew high into the air and floated below the ceiling out of reach. Susan retaliated by aiming a kick at Gloria that sent her crashing into the opposite wall. She slid down in an unconscious heap. Before Gemah could react, Susan reached into her pocket and pointed the Subjugator at her.

"I'll kill you this time," she warned. "Give me the gun."

The gun turned and pointed at Susan. In response, Susan lifted the Subjugator her finger poised over the button. They stared at each other.

Chris came to just in time to see the sole of Elle's foot above his face. He rolled out of the way as she stomped. She missed and lost her balance. He delivered a blow to the back of her knee. Elle collapsed on top of him. He rolled with her and pinned her under him. They struggled. She tried to gouge his eyes. He had his hands around her neck and squeezed. They fought in grim silence. Finally, her arms fell away from him. He carefully released the pressure on her throat ready to reapply it should she resume the fight. She was unconscious. He got up, found his weapon, and ran off in the direction of the gun shot.

"If I press the button, you'll drop like a stone and I'll get my gun anyway," Susan said. "So you might as well hand it over."
Gemah had to admit this was sound reasoning. She hated feeling so helpless. The gun turned in mid-air and gently floated toward Susan. She caught it and pointed it at the unconscious Gloria.
"No!" Gemah shrieked.
A man appeared in the doorway his gun pointed at Susan. "Drop it!"
Susan looked up. "Chris! How nice to see you again. I thought I'd left you in a ditch."
"Nice try."
"How did you find this place?" Susan asked.
"I planted a tracking device on Gemah during the dance lesson."
"Very clever. I'll have to make sure to cut it out of her after we leave here."
"You're not leaving. Drop your gun, Susan."
Susan raised her hands as in defeat and put the gun on the floor. As she came up, she grabbed Gemah in one swift movement and held up the Subjugator.
Chris moved forward but Susan yelled "Stop!"
Chris froze.
"Gemah, explain to your gym teacher what this little device is capable of."

84

"It's called a Subjugator. She can render me unconscious with it."

"Or kill her," Susan finished. "If you want Gemah to live, you'll get out of our way now."

Susan stepped forward pushing Gemah ahead of her.

Suddenly Chris was pushed into the room, fell over Leung's body and crashed into Gemah who was knocked backwards into Susan. The three of them went down in a heap of arms and legs. Elle entered the room and attacked Chris for a second time. Her kick missed him and hit Susan's hand. The Subjugator went flying. Susan shoved Gemah off her and crawled after the device.

Chris turned and fought with Elle. Gemah scuttled backwards to avoid being kicked. As she tried to get up, she realized that she couldn't put weight on her left leg. Her ankle was in excruciating pain.

Suddenly there was a gun shot. Everyone froze. Susan pointed Chris' gun at him. He stood holding a dying Elle in his arms.

"Damn! I meant to get you, not her," Susan said coolly. "Oh, well." She shot again. The bullet made a ninety degree turn and hit the ceiling above his head.

"Gemah!" Susan screamed in frustration.

Before she had a chance to try again, they heard footsteps running towards them. Susan hurtled from the room.

"Get her!" Chris shouted at his men when they entered the room. Susan had a head start and knew her way around the compound. Chris gently lowered Elle's body to the floor.

85

"Stay here," he said to Gemah. "I'll be back." He ran off after his men.

Gemah looked around. The room was completely destroyed. Elle and Dr. Leung were dead. She crawled past them towards Gloria. She was pale and her breathing was shallow. Suddenly Gemah remembered the Subjugator. Had Susan taken it? Gemah concentrated her x-ray vision on the rubble of broken furniture. She found Susan's gun under the broken bed, but there was no sign of the device. Gemah leaned against the wall beside Gloria. She felt completely drained.

Chapter 12

"Please sit." John walked around his desk and pulled up chairs for Gemah and Gloria. He noted that both looked much better than they did two weeks ago when he had visited them in hospital. The door opened and Chris entered.

Once everyone was seated, John began, "I brought you here so we can jointly put the pieces together. In order for us to help you, I need complete honesty. Gemah, I know you've been through a terrible ordeal, but even the smallest detail might be of importance, so please try to remember everything that's happened."

Gemah nodded.

"What I'm about to tell you is classified. However, I feel that you need this knowledge to help you make sense of the situation. Here's what we know," John said, "15 years ago, a secret organization formed by the CIA was tasked to experiment on human GMOs. Two years into their research, the CIA got Intel about a crashed alien craft in the Atlantic. All five pilots on board were dead. The CIA recovered the bodies and brought them to the GMO research center. The scientists discovered that the alien DNA was closely linked to that of Earth's dolphins. The researchers speculated that the aliens had seeded our oceans millennia ago and used the dolphins to monitor our activity. By visiting Earth and debriefing the dolphins, the aliens got a good picture of our level of technology, industrialization, pollution and climate change. During the autopsy on the aliens, the scientists discovered devices implanted in their brains. They surmised that these implants boost brain power and aid in communication as the aliens' vocal chords were atrophied. The GMO experiment was changed to include alien DNA in an effort to create a humanoid able to communicate with the aliens when they returned."

John paused to take a sip from his coffee before he continued: "This brings us to Walter. He was a senior CIA agent with top clearance. He recruited you." John inclined his head towards Gloria. "Walter was also a man of science. He had retired from service, but returned for the opportunity to work on this project. With his security clearance and former track record, he had no problems getting his hands on the Intel. Realizing the precarious nature of the research, he decided to collect evidence he could use as leverage should he need it."

"But he gave it to me, when I ran off with Gemah," Gloria interrupted.

"Yes, he gave it to you and alerted us hoping we would find you before the CIA did. That part worked out. Unfortunately, it cost him his life." There was a moment of silence.

"Gemah disappeared off the radar until the incident at Discovery Cove," John continued. "We realized that the CIA would come looking for her and put Chris in charge of finding her." John turned and spoke to Gemah.

"We made a deal with Dr. Barnes offering him funding for the school in return for hiring Chris as a teacher. Barnes arranged a leave of absence for the school's Phys. Ed teacher, Mrs. Cullen, and created a position for Chris. What we didn't know is that Barnes also made a deal with the CIA and hired Susan Walsh as a counselor. Chris' assignment was to keep you safe. As a precaution he planted a tracking device in your back that would allow us to find you in case you were abducted. By the way, it was your friend Sarah who alerted Chris."

Gemah nodded. "I couldn't think of what to do. I sent her a message."

"It worked," Chris said. "I arrived in Susan's office just as the paramedics were loading you up. I came in the ambulance with you, but they knocked me out and dumped me at a truck stop. Not one of my finer moments," he added wryly.

"And now, Gemah," John continued, "We need you to fill in the blanks for us. What happened when you woke up?"

Gemah told them about the telepathy and telekinesis tests, Elle's combat training, and the punishments with the Subjugator.

"They took blood from me," she said. "Susan told me that I was engineered to be a super-weapon to be deployed by the US in special situations. She said they had the other brain implant devices and wanted to clone me. But...," and here Gemah frowned, "Susan said I had dolphin DNA. She said nothing about alien DNA."

John nodded. "That's because she didn't know about it. Susan Walsh, or CIA operative Hunt, is actually a double agent. Her real name is Yokovski, and she works for the SVR. They believe that the US is creating a new and powerful weapon, a way to spy on Russia. So I'm sure Yokovski's plan was to take you back to Russia, continue your training, and use you as a weapon."

John turned to Chris. "Did we recover blood samples at the compound?"

"No. She must have taken them."

"Damn! That means the Russians can produce four more GEMAHs."

Chris broke the silence. "If they succeed, I'm sure we can handle it."

"No you can't," Gemah said. Chris and John were lifted out of their chairs and pinned against the wall. "Gemah!" Gloria cried out in shock.

"This is what you're up against. I could kill you with a single thought." Chris felt his throat constrict for a moment before he was settled back into his chair and everything returned to normal.

"I am a weapon," Gemah said sadly. "But I was raised with love and compassion. These clones won't be."

John and Chris looked shaken.

"Thank you for that demonstration, Gemah," John said. "I think you've just made it clear that keeping you safe is of the utmost importance."

"I can look after myself," Gemah said, "The only thing that can stop me, and them, is the Subjugator."

"Where did that thing go?" John asked.

"We've looked everywhere," Chris said. "I think Susan got away with it. We pursued her through the compound, but she was prepped for an escape. She had a helicopter waiting by the back door."

"That's it then," John said. "All we can do is wait and see if they succeed in cloning Gemah."

John pulled some paperwork from his desk drawer.

"In the meantime, we've spoken to CSIS, the Canadian Security Intelligence Service. We've convinced them to help us keep you safe. Your best chance at a normal life is in rural Canada, away from the CIA. If the SVR comes looking for you, they'll search in the U.S. and we'll get wind of it."

John handed the passports and immigration papers to Gloria and Gemah. "You are mother and daughter now."

Gemah opened her passport. She stared at it. "My name is Nancy, after my mother."

Gemah looked up at John. "Thank you."

Gloria turned to Gemah and smiled.

"Nice to meet you, Nancy. I'm Jillian."

"When are we leaving?" Gemah asked.

"Now," Chris answered. "I'll be your escort across the border."

They got up and shook hands with John.

"Jill and Nancy, welcome to Canada and a new life!"

*** End ***

Dear Reader,

I hope you've enjoyed 'Gifted'. Please leave a review on Amazon.com and help me create more books for you to enjoy.

'Chronicles of the Imagination' is a series of unrelated science fiction and fiction short stories. The second book in the series, 'Sanctuary', is the story of a young indigenous girl, Keisha, living deep in the Amazon forest. One night, as the tribe is gathered round their cooking fires, they see a star fall from the sky. Keisha is mysteriously drawn to the fallen star. When she sets out to investigate, her life is changed forever.

Visit https://www.zoheretbooks.com/dzadamsbooks to get the next book in the series.

Happy reading!
D.Z. Adams